Dragon
Pancake Party!

Adapted by Mara Conlon
Based on an original TV episode written by Steven Westren

SCHOLASTIC INC.

New York   Toronto   London   Auckland
Sydney   Mexico City   New Delhi   Hong Kong

ISBN: 978-0-439-78501-3

Published by Scholastic Inc. SCHOLASTIC and associated logos
are trademarks and/or registered trademarks of Scholastic Inc.

12 11 10 9 8 7 6 5 4 3 2 1   10 11 12 13 14/0

Printed in the U.S.A.   40
First printing, January 2010

"Grumble," went Dragon's tummy.
He was hungry!
"What should I eat for breakfast?"

"I know," Dragon said.
"I will make tasty pancakes!"

Then Dragon had an idea.
"I will invite my friends
to a pancake party!" he said.

"Dude, I love pancakes,"
said Alligator.

Ostrich and Mailmouse
would come too.

Beaver said he had never
had pancakes.

But he told Dragon he would come.

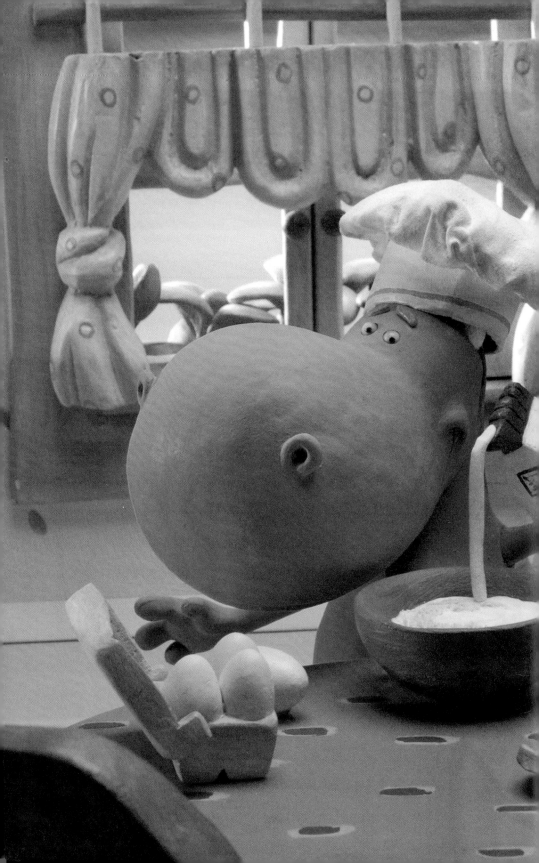

"I have not made pancakes in a long time," said Dragon. "I should practice!"

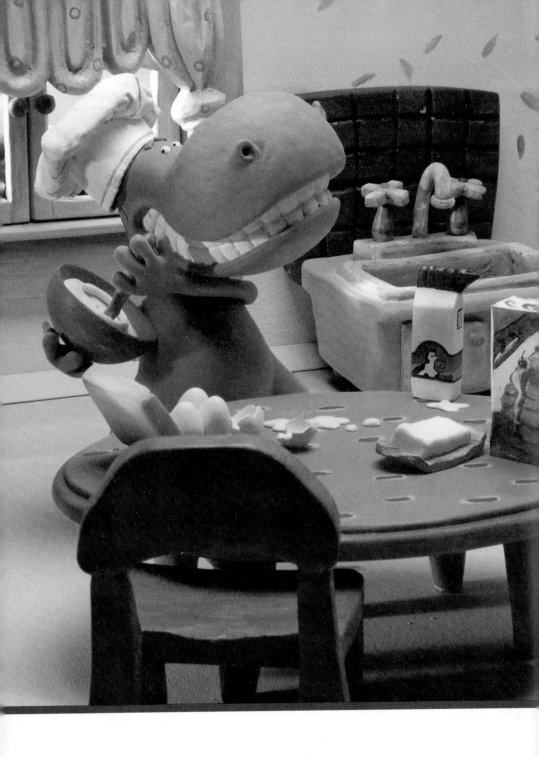

Dragon made the batter.
That was easy.

Then he tried to flip a pancake.
That was not so easy.

One landed in the sink.

One landed on the fridge.

Two landed on the chair!

"I *flip* the pancakes," he said.
"They *fly*!" He giggled.

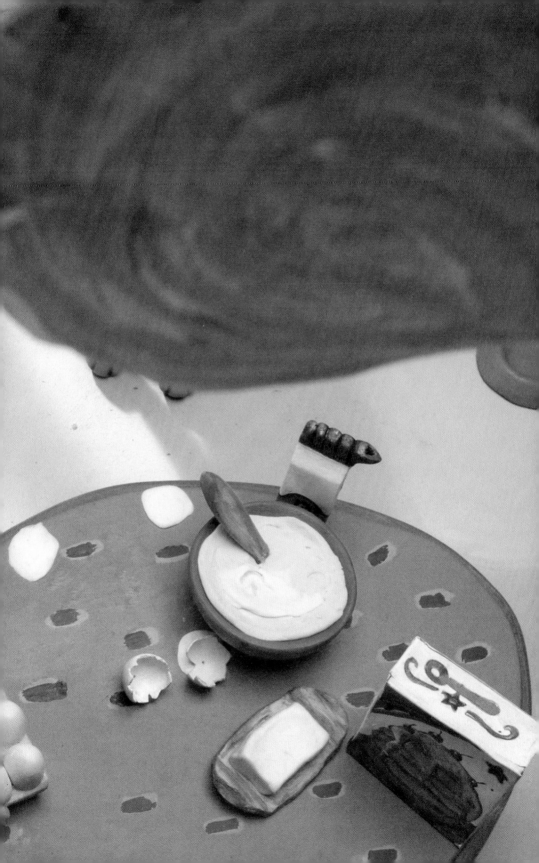

Next Dragon tried to pour syrup.
What a sticky mess!

Then he tried to make lots of pancakes at the same time. What a mushy mess!

Dragon kept trying.
When the pancakes were perfect,
he called his friends.
"Dig in!" said Dragon.

Everyone ate the pancakes.
Everyone except Beaver.
"Are your pancakes too hot?"
asked Mailmouse.

"No," said Beaver.
"I don't know if I will
like them."

"Trying new things is fun," said Dragon.
"Like ice cream," Alligator said.
"And chocolate!" Mailmouse added.

"I guess it can't hurt," said Beaver.
He took one bite, and then another.

"These are great!" he said.

"I know what we should try next,"
said Dragon.

Dragon laughed.
"Let's make *more* pancakes!" he said.

"Yup," Beaver said.
"And let's eat more, too!"